DUMP TRUCK TROUBLE

By **Mary Tillworth**
Illustrated by **MJ Illustrations**

Based on the teleplay "Construction Psyched!"
by **Michael Rubiner** and **Bob Mittenthal**

A Random House PICTUREBACK® Book

Random House 🏠 New York

© 2014 Viacom International Inc. All rights reserved. Published in the United States by Random House Children's Books,
a division of Random House, Inc., 1745 Broadway, New York, NY 10019, and in Canada by Random House of Canada Limited, Toronto.
Pictureback, Random House, and the Random House colophon are registered trademarks of Random House, Inc. Nickelodeon,
Bubble Guppies, and all related titles, logos, and characters are trademarks of Viacom International Inc.
randomhouse.com/kids
ISBN 978-0-385-37526-9
MANUFACTURED IN CHINA
10 9 8 7 6 5 4 3 2

One sunny morning, Gil and Goby were playing in the park.
"*Vroom! Vroom!*" rumbled Goby as he pushed his dump truck.
Gil dug through the sand with his bulldozer. Suddenly, he heard
honking sounds coming from the other side of a big fence! "Whoa!"
he said. "Check this out, Goby!"

"It's a construction site!" Goby exclaimed. "Look—there's a dump truck! And a bulldozer! And a crane!"

Gil and Goby wanted to share their discovery with the rest of the Bubble Guppies. They raced to school.

When Goby and Gil got to class, they told their teacher, Mr. Grouper, about the construction site.

"There was a bulldozer just like mine!" said Gil, holding up his toy.

"And there was a dump truck just like— Oh, no! I forgot my dump truck!" Goby cried.

Mr. Grouper led the Bubble Guppies back to the construction site. Goby's dump truck was nowhere to be found!

"Let's go ask if anyone has seen your dump truck," suggested Gil.

"Excuse me," Mr. Grouper called to one of the construction workers. "Have you seen a toy dump truck around here?"

"No, I'm sorry, I haven't," a construction worker named Liz replied. "But I'll sure keep an eye out for it."

"Construction vehicles are cool," said Nonny.

"What does 'vehicle' mean?" asked Oona.

"A vehicle is something that carries or moves things," replied Nonny.

"There are many different kinds of construction vehicles," explained Mr. Grouper. "The one that pushes piles of dirt and rocks is called a bulldozer. Dump trucks carry stuff, and the really tall one that lifts things high into the air is called a crane."

The Bubble Guppies returned to school, talking excitedly about construction vehicles.

Back in class, Goby couldn't stop worrying about his toy dump truck. So later that day, Mr. Grouper took the Guppies on a field trip to look for Goby's toy.

When they arrived, the construction site had become a rodeo!

Liz the construction worker was now the rodeo's announcer. "Welcome to the Bubbletucky Construction Rodeo!" she said. "Excuse me. Did you find my friend's dump truck?" asked Gil. "Nobody's been able to find it," Liz replied sadly. "But you boys go enjoy the rodeo, and afterward, we'll see what we can do."

The Bubble Guppies watched dump trucks, bulldozers, and cranes zoom around the rodeo ring. For the big finale, three dump trucks dumped sand into big piles in front of three holes in the ground.

"Get ready for El Dozer!" Liz announced. "He is going to put those piles of sand into those holes!"

As El Dozer bulldozed the sand piles into the holes, Gil and Goby noticed a toy dump truck sticking out of the third hole.

"Stop the rodeo!" shouted Gil. "Goby's dump truck—it's down there!"

Liz leapt up. "Come with me!" she called.

With Gil and Goby close behind, Liz climbed into the rodeo ring. She jumped into a crane. Just before El Dozer pushed the third sand pile into the last hole, Liz lowered the crane claw and scooped up Goby's toy dump truck!

"Thank you for saving my truck!" Goby said to Liz.
"You're welcome!" she replied.
Soon Gil and Goby were back in the sand. Goby pushed his dump truck over a hill. "Dump truck coming through!" he said happily.

"This is the best doghouse ever!" said Gil.
"Arf! Arf!" Bubble Puppy agreed.

Gil beamed. "Bubble Puppy loves his new doghouse!" he exclaimed.

Bubble Puppy swam up to the top of his home and tooted the horn. *"Arf! Arf!"* he barked.

After they were done, Molly and Gil showed Bubble Puppy the doghouse. "What do you think of your new home?" they asked him.

Working together, the Bubble Guppies, Mr. Grouper, and the construction workers built a *fin*-tastic doghouse for Bubble Puppy! On top, they built a balcony with a little horn to toot. There was even a slide that wrapped around the house and ended at a pool at the bottom!

Then Mr. Grouper hammered nails into the boards. When he was done, he had made one side of Bubble Puppy's doghouse!

To build the top of the doghouse, a construction worker cut boards into different sizes. Then he put them together to make a triangle frame. Using wrenches, Goby and the worker bolted the boards together.

Gil and Molly invited the rest of the Bubble Guppies and Mr. Grouper to the construction site to help build Bubble Puppy's doghouse. When they arrived, all the Bubble Guppies put on hard hats to be safe.

A construction worker showed Oona and Gil the plan for the doghouse. "Before we start, we check the blueprint to make sure we've planned everything right," he said.

It was time to start! Molly and Oona held a piece of wood while a worker sawed through it. He cut the wood into boards of the same length.

"Don't forget the paint!" said Deema, handing them a bucket.
"And your tools!" added Goby, pointing to a tool board.

Gil and Molly went to Deema and
Goby's hardware store, where they found
all the supplies they needed to build
Bubble Puppy's doghouse.

First the workers drew a plan for Bubble Puppy's doghouse. "This is called a blueprint," one of them explained.

Once the blueprint was finished, the workers told Gil and Molly that they needed to go to the hardware store for supplies.

At the construction site, Gil and Molly met some construction workers. They wore bright yellow vests and hard hats.

"Will you help us build a doghouse for Bubble Puppy?" Gil asked.

"Of course!" said the construction workers.

"Hey, Gil! How's it going?" Molly asked.

"Great!" replied Gil. "But I have a big project to do today. I want to build Bubble Puppy a doghouse."

"Remember that construction site we visited? Maybe we can ask some construction workers for help!" Molly suggested.

One day, Gil was playing fetch with Bubble Puppy.

LET'S BUILD A DOGHOUSE!

Adapted by **Mary Tillworth**
Cover illustrated by **Sue DiCicco** and **Steve Talkowski**
Interior illustrated by **MJ Illustrations**

Based on the teleplay "Build Me a Building!"
by **Adam Peltzman**

A Random House PICTUREBACK® Book

Random House 🏠 New York

© 2014 Viacom International Inc. All rights reserved. Published in the United States by Random House Children's Books,
a division of Random House, Inc., 1745 Broadway, New York, NY 10019, and in Canada by Random House of Canada Limited, Toronto.
Pictureback, Random House, and the Random House colophon are registered trademarks of Random House, Inc.
Originally published in slightly different form as *The Best Doghouse Ever!* in the United States by Random House in 2003.
Nickelodeon, Bubble Guppies, and all related titles, logos, and characters are trademarks of Viacom International Inc.
randomhouse.com/kids
ISBN 978-0-385-37526-9
MANUFACTURED IN CHINA
10 9 8 7 6 5 4 3 2